Topsy + Tim

Learn abc

Jean and Gareth Adamson

Aa

anorak

In winter, when the wind's like ice,
Anoraks are warm and nice.

Bb
balloon

Balloons are fun – until they burst!

This time Topsy came off worst.

Cc
caravan

A caravan's a lovely way
Of going on a holiday.

Dd

dinosaur

Topsy and Tim know where to find
Dinosaurs that are quiet and kind.

Ee

egg

What has Tim found? Yes, you've guessed:
Easter eggs in a cosy nest.

Ff

firemen

Firemen to a fire are dashing,
Siren wailing, blue lights flashing.

Gg

gate

Country gates keep cows from harm.

Don't leave them open on the farm.

Hh

hand

See what Topsy and Tim have done –
Hand print patterns to give to Mum.

Ii

igloo

An igloo for two would be nice
In a land that is all snow and ice.

Jj
jumble

At a jumble sale you'll find
Funny clothes of every kind.

Kk

kite

The wind is tugging at Tim's kite.

Now he has to hold on tight.

Ll

lolly

Ice creams are licky. Lollies are lickier.

Ice creams are sticky but lollies are stickier.

Mm

mouse

Can you help find Tubby Mouse?

He is somewhere around the house.

Nn

nurse

Oh, Nurse Topsy, do be quick!
I think that Tim is feeling sick.

Oo

orange

Orange tastes lovely drunk through a straw.

Soon Topsy and Tim will be ready for more!

Pp

puppy

Roly the puppy is brown as a bun.

Rolling with Roly is wonderful fun.

Qq
queen

Topsy is queen so Tim bows down,

But it's Tim's turn next to wear the crown.

Rr

rabbit

Rabbits like oats and grass to eat,

With carrots for a special treat.

Ss

slide

Slowly – climb – the – steps – and – then...
Swoosh! You're sliding down again.

Tt
tractor

Tractors are slow, tractors are strong.
Tractors pull big loads along.

Uu

umbrella

Your umbrella is a walking roof.

In rain it keeps you waterproof... nearly!

V v

vet

Mr NcNab, the best of vets,

Will always help to cure sick pets.

Ww

water

Topsy loves the water spray.

It keeps her cool on a summer's day.

Xx

x-ray

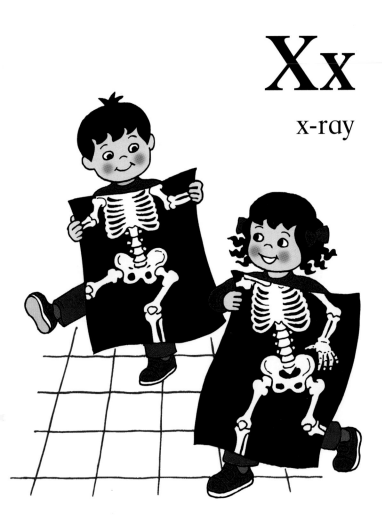

Inside you and inside me
Are bones that x-ray photos see.

Yy

yawn

When Topsy yawns, so does Tim,

And seeing them makes me begin.

Zz

zebra

Zebra doesn't care who wins

When playing football with the twins.

Aa Bb Cc

Gg Hh Ii

Ll Mm

Qq Rr Ss

Vv Ww